Click, Clack, Peep!

Doreen Cronin

Illustrated by **Betsy Lewin**

SIMON AND SCHUSTER

London   New York   Sydney   Toronto   New Delhi

SIMON AND SCHUSTER

First published in Great Britain in 2015 by Simon and Schuster UK Ltd

1st Floor, 222 Gray's Inn Road, London, WC1X 8HB • A CBS Company • Published in the USA in 2015 by Atheneum Books for Young Readers, an imprint of Simon and Schuster Children's Publishing Division, New York • Text copyright © 2015 by Doreen Cronin • Illustrations copyright © 2015 by Betsy Lewin. • All rights reserved. • The right of Doreen Cronin and Betsy Lewin to be identified as the author and illustrator of this work has been asserted by them in accordance with the Copyright, Designs and Patents Act, 1988 • All rights reserved, including the right of reproduction in whole or in part in any form • A CIP catalogue record for this book is available from the British Library upon request • ISBN: 978-1-4711-2484-6 • Printed in China 10 9 8 7 6 5 4 3 2 1 • www.simonandschuster.co.uk

For Betsy and Ted
—D. C.

For little Ellis,
the newest "peep" in the Lewin clan
—B. L.

Click, Clack, peep!

Farmer Brown stuck his head out the window.
The farm was too quiet.
Everyone was watching the egg.

Not a moo.
Not a click.

Not an oink.
Not a clack.

Not a baa.
Not a cluck.
Not a thing.

Then . . . a crack.

Inside the barn
everyone gathered closer.

Baby Duck!

Baby Duck laughed.
PEEP PEEP PEEP
And laughed again.

Baby Duck waddled.
PEEP PEEP PEEP
And waddled again.

Baby Duck played.
PEEP PEEP PEEP
And played again!

The animals yawned.

peep peep peep

And yawned again.

The chickens sang a lullaby.

But Baby Duck would not sleep.

peep

peep

peep

The cows lowered the shades.

But Baby Duck would not sleep.

peep peep peep

The sheep knitted a blanket.

But Baby Duck would not sleep.

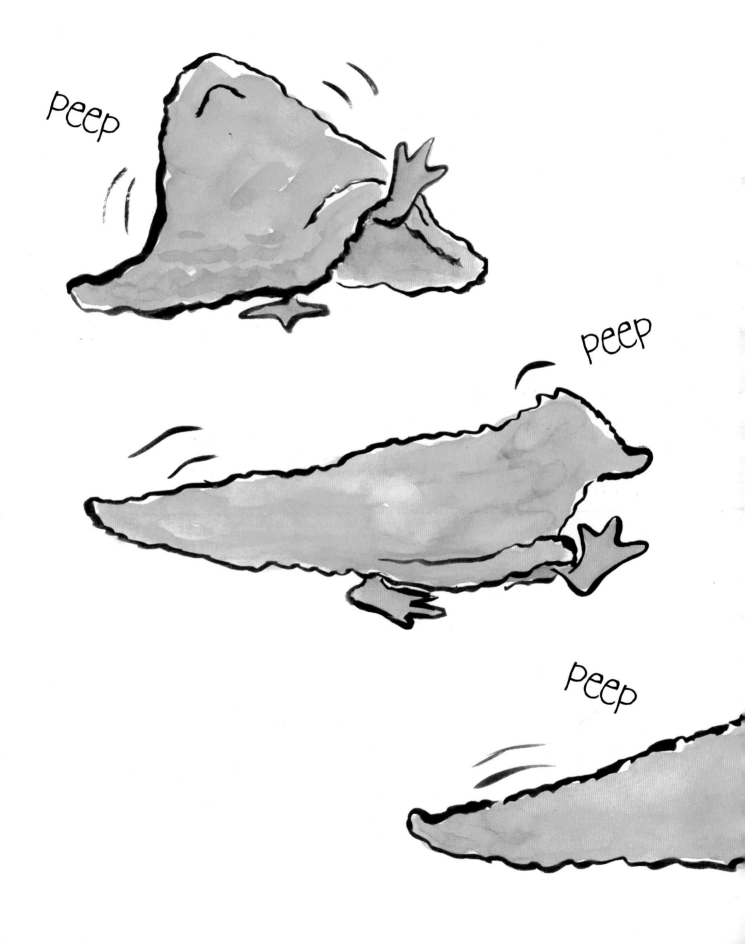

The chickens went outside to get some sleep.
The cows went outside to get some sleep.

The sheep went outside to get some sleep.
The mice went outside to get some sleep.

Duck took off his headphones.

peep
peep
peep

He put Baby Duck
into a bucket.

peep peep peep

He covered her
with a blanket.

peep peep peep

He carried her outside.

peep peep peep

He climbed
into
the tractor.

peep peep peep

He buckled up the seat belts.

peep peep peep

And backed out of the barnyard.

beep beep beep

He drove
back and forth.

peep
peep
peep

Back and forth.

peep peep peep

Back and forth.

peep, peep . . .

Farmer Brown opens his eyes
after a good night's sleep.

Not a moo.
Not a cluck.
Not a clack.

Not a peep.